The Philadelphia Inquirer

The Big Hustle

A Novella by
George Anastasia

Cover and illustrations by Gregory Manchess

Books by The Philadelphia Inquirer

Lost at Sea:
The Atlantic Claims 10 Men
By Douglas A. Campbell

Crisis on the Coast:
The Risky Development of America's Shore
By Gilbert M. Gaul and Anthony R. Wood

Beyond the Flames:
One toxic dump, two decades of sorrow
By Susan Q. Stranahan and Larry King

FAQs:
Sound answers to real computing questions
By John J. Fried

Playing A Round:
The guide to Philadelphia-area golf courses
By Joe Logan

ISBN 1-58822-009-5

Introduction

It is one of the most frequently quoted pieces of literary advice. "Write what you know," they say.

"The Big Hustle" is what I know.

In the spring of 2000, an editor at The Inquirer Sunday magazine asked if I would be interested in writing the magazine's summer fiction series, a four-part literary work that in the past had been farmed out to different writers each week. The idea was to present a story in serial form, something that had a local angle and that might resonate with readers.

For several years, I had been toying with an idea for a story, never putting it on paper, but thinking about it occasionally as I wrote other things.

It was about the mob and casino gambling and, of course, Atlantic City.

I've always been fascinated with Atlantic City. When I was growing up, I spent part of every summer there. This was back in the 1950s and early 1960s. My grandmother had a house on South Bellevue Avenue, a block and a half from the Boardwalk. Atlantic City was a different place then. I once wrote an essay about that for the magazine. The piece ran in 1988 on the 10th anniversary of the opening of the first casino. It was a remembrance of a better time, a time that probably only existed in the mind of a child.

Here is a part of that essay:

I think about my grandmother's home a block from the Boardwalk ... and about the smell of spaghetti sauce (we call it gravy) floating on the breeze as I walk back from the beach on a Sunday afternoon.

A Phillies game would be blaring on someone's radio. They were losing, of course, a group of aging Whiz Kids kept together a little too long, struggling against the powerful Dodgers of Brooklyn and the upstart Braves of Milwaukee.

All along the block there would be streams of water running out of alleys, across pristine sidewalks and into the street, the water coming from outdoor showers where bathers washed the sand off their feet and legs before climbing the stairs that led to the second-floor porches of most of the homes.

It was always hot and warm and sunny and clean on South Bellevue Avenue then. And in front of a small, street-level apartment in the middle of the block there was an Italian water ice stand. Real Italian water ice. One flavor, lemon. With tiny bits of the rind still in the ice ... .

On the corner of Bellevue and Pacific ... was a grocery store, and every evening around 5, earlier and more often on weekends, a local bakery would deliver bags and bags of hot, crisp Italian bread.

I remember standing on that corner, tanned and scrubbed clean after a day at the beach, my hair wet and combed back, waiting with a quarter in my hand for the baker to arrive, then jockeying for a position in the tiny, crowded grocery store to buy a loaf of that bread still hot from the oven ... Today the grocery store is a 24-hour massage parlor. The water ice stand is long gone.

Memories, of course, tend to soften all the edges.

Casino gambling didn't change the Atlantic City of my childhood. Its demise had started long before ...

I liked it better when the Dodgers were in Brooklyn and the Braves were in Milwaukee and you could smell the gravy on a Sunday afternoon.

Until *The Big Hustle*, that essay, called *The Past Resort*, generated more reader response than anything I had written during my 26 years at The Inquirer.

It was what I knew.

In my mind, there has always been something charming about Atlantic City. Historically, it's been a haven for assorted rogues and scoundrels, but their act was more *Guys and Dolls* than *Goodfellas*. The coming of casinos brought a bigger layer of glitz and glitter, but underneath I still saw the resort of my childhood.

In 1976, The Inquirer sent me down there to help cover the casino gambling referendum. I spent most of the next decade tracking the impact that legalized gaming had on the city. I wrote pieces about the land speculators who turned the city into a Monopoly board and about hookers who turned Pacific Avenue into a bordello, stories about high rollers who arrived in Lear Jets and bet thousands of dollars on a hand of blackjack and about blue-haired ladies who came by bus and who could turn $10 in nickels into a day-trip.

What struck me as I watched it all unfold was that casino gambling hadn't changed the way the game was played in Atlantic City. It just made the pot bigger.

Now it's roulette and black jack and gaudy gaming halls. Before it was bingo parlors and back room casinos. The point is, there have always been people looking for a piece of the action, looking for an edge, looking for a way to cut the odds. People whose entire life is a hustle.

This story is about them. And as I reread it in preparation for its publication in this form, I hear their voices again and I see and feel the places that were so much a part of me.

Frankie Bello, Nicky Botts, Vinny Barbano, Little Paulie Scarpino, Rita Manoff and the beautiful Julia are based in part on those I knew and met either as a kid or while writing about Atlantic City and the mob for The Inquirer.

The Big Hustle is a combination casino caper and love story. Think of it as *The Sopranos* meets *Moonstruck.*

It's what I know.

— George Anasastia
September 2001

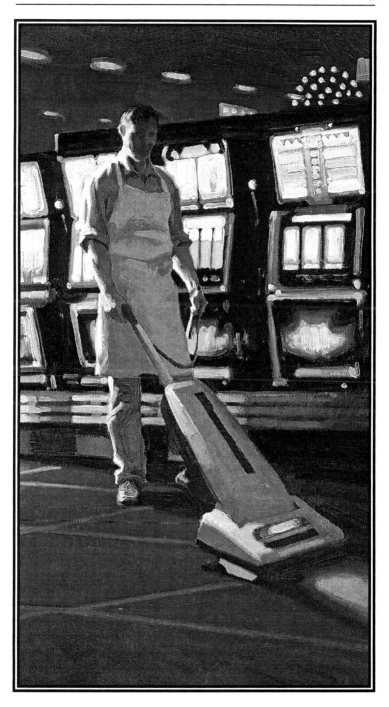

Chapter 1

A ntonio Alvarez won a free trip to the Bahamas for himself and his family on the morning of March 7, 1979. It happened in the baccarat pit of the Renaissance Casino Hotel. Alvarez was cleaning the floor at the time.

The casino was closed. The smell of stale smoke, cheap whiskey and warm beer hung in the air. "Disco Inferno" was blaring from the sound system in the cocktail lounge where a dozen hollow-eyed gamblers in wrinkled clothes were sipping coffee. This was back before they permitted 24-hour gambling on the Boardwalk, back before Atlantic City gave up any pretense of being something other than Las Vegas East.

Casinos used to close between 6 a.m. and 10 a.m. in the early days of the great gambling experiment. This was to give a gambler a chance to catch his breath, clear his head, and maybe come to his senses before he blew this week's paycheck, next month's mortgage, or the deed to the house.

In the beginning, legalized gambling was steeped in

this type of phony compassion for the little guy. Politicians would tell you with a straight face that casinos were a "means to an end, not an end in themselves;" that they were going to be part of a "unique form of urban renewal." It's right there in the legislation. You could look it up.

Antonio Alvarez, who lived in a third-floor walkup in the South Inlet with his pregnant wife, Yolanda, and their two little boys, Miguel and Juan, was supposed to be one of the beneficiaries of this social experiment. He was making $220 a week as part of the maintenance crew at the Renaissance, the city's first, and at this particular time, only casino.

Opportunity was what the politicians sold when they went out and beat the drums for casino gambling three years earlier. And opportunity is what Tonio Alvarez found that morning. Under a baccarat table. In the VIP pit where gamblers bet a minimum of $100 a hand.

It was the kind of thing Tonio used to daydream about as he pushed the high-powered vacuum cleaner over the casino's crimson carpet. He'd go through the numbers, doing the math in his head — $100 per hand minimum, at least 50 hands an hour, five players at the table. It came to $25,000 an hour, minimum. Probably a hell of a lot more.

Alvarez would have to work more than two years to earn what that one table generated in an hour.

Minimum.

Then his vacuum cleaner struck something. Alvarez

hit the switch to shut off the machine, knelt and looked under the table. He saw a blue and white Addidas gym bag. His first thought was that some drunken gambler had left it behind and that he might get a reward for finding it. He casually reached under the table, grabbed one of the straps and pulled the bag out.

He opened it. Then he froze. For a minute he knelt there staring at the contents. Then, moving very slowly, he reached for the security beeper that every worker had to wear whenever they were on the casino floor. Sweat was beading on Tonio Alvarez's back. His lightly starched, blue uniform shirt was sticking to his skin. His face, he knew, was glistening.

―――

"We want to keep this as quiet as possible," said the man pacing behind the mahogany desk in the big corner office on the 12th floor of the casino hotel. "I think the reasons are obvious."

"And they would be?"

The man stopped pacing, looked up at the ceiling and sighed.

"They told me, Mister Bello, that you would be difficult. They also told me that you were good. So far, they're half right."

Frankie Bello smiled.

"Sounds like somebody knows me pretty good," he said.

Bello was sitting in a large, black leather couch that he figured was worth more than all the furniture in his four-room apartment.

"Here's the thing," he said, leaning forward and poking the air with his forefinger for emphasis. "You called me, I didn't call you. You got a problem here. Maybe I could help. But I gotta know where you're comin' from. Else I'll get lost. Or just run around in circles.

"I know this place is a money machine, but I don't think you or your shareholders want to just throw cash away. You wanna pay me $400 a day, which is almost three times my rate. That's fine. But strange as it might sound, I don't wanna waste your money. Or my time. I earn what I make. That's just the way it is."

The gym bag sat on an expensive coffee table in front of Bello. Its contents were spread out before him: three sticks of dynamite, a cheap remote control detonator, some wire and the note. Bello picked it up and read the large, neat block letters again. NEXT TIME WE CONNECT ALL THE PIECES. BOOM! WAIT FOR OUR CALL. 7 P.M.

Bello noticed a little curly line through the middle of the seven. Very European. Or maybe just an affectation. Other than that, there was nothing unusual about the writing.

"We haven't alerted the Division of Gaming Enforcement because we don't want any publicity about this," said G. Malcolm Bradley, the president and CEO of Renaissance Casinos Inc. "We want to handle it in-house — but with your assistance, of course."

"Of course," said Bello, who was about to crack wise

again, but thought better of it.

"I want you to work with our chief of security, Tom Sistrunk," Bradley added quickly. "I think you two were with the ACPD at the same time."

"Sure," Bello said dryly. "Tommy and me go back."

"Good. I'm hoping between the two of you, we can settle this quickly and quietly. Obviously, these people, whoever they are, are trying to extort the casino."

"Obviously," said Bello, trying not to sound sarcastic.

Five minutes later, Frankie Bello was in an elevator heading for the lobby of the casino-hotel.

It was clear from his conversation with Bradley that this operation had to be run off the books. The casino wanted the bomb threat kept quiet for the simplest of all reasons, Bradley said. It didn't want to scare away customers. With the casino pulling in several million dollars a day, that was understandable.

You call in the authorities and right away you run the risk of somebody leaking it to the press. Then you've got all kinds of headaches that you don't need. Maybe even some wild-eyed politician suggesting that you close down for a day or two.

The Renaissance, as the only game in town, had a license to print money. And Bradley wasn't about to give that up, bomb or no bomb.

But why, out of all the private investigators in the city, did the Renaissance people call him? Bello was sure Sistrunk was the reason. Bello would be the point man, the guy who got his hands dirty. And Sistrunk would be the one to grab the glory, just like when they worked in the detective bureau.

Sistrunk headed the squad for five years. Bello was one of the unit's top investigators. Together they made dozens of cases. But Bello, because he was usually working undercover, stayed in the background when it was time for an arrest to be made. Bello was the one who got down in the muck with the pimps, the prostitutes, the drugged-out coke heads and the wannabe wiseguys. Sistrunk was the one who stood front and center for the newspaper photographers and the television cameras.

Now they were about the run the drill again.

Bello had quit the department because he didn't like working for people like Tommy Sistrunk. But for $400 a day he figured he'd give it one more shot. There was, however, something else about the Bradley conversation that bothered him. He was sure there was some other reason Bradley didn't want the state poking around.

It was 11 a.m. when Bello stepped out of the elevator and walked onto the floor of the casino. The joint was already packed. People were three-deep around the craps tables. There wasn't an empty seat at any of the blackjack tables. Even the baccarat pits, where during the day the minimum bet was $25, were busy. And the noise. Bello was always amazed by the noise, by the way it played tricks on your senses. The din from the slot machines was so constant that if you spent two or three minutes on the casino floor, you stopped hearing it. It became more a color than a sound, part of the bright, shiny backdrop.

Bello looked at the crowd, shook his head in dismay and headed for the Boardwalk. He needed air and time to think. He had a copy of the note in his pocket and an appointment with Sistrunk at 1 p.m. That gave him two hours to do a little preliminary work. He knew where he wanted to start.

As he headed for the revolving doors that led to the Boardwalk he saw a familiar face coming toward him.

"Frankie, my main man. What's up?"

"Not much, Nick. How ya been?"

Nicholas "Nicky Botts" Carlucci was dressed in jeans, a Philadelphia Eagles tee-shirt and a red baseball cap with the words "Doggy Man" scrawled in yellow across the brim. He had a wad of bills, fives, tens and twenties, in his hand.

"I'm doin' good," Botts said.

"Selling hot dogs on the Boardwalk?"

"Hey, it's legit."

"Sure, Nick," Bello said with a smile, "and everybody in here is breakin' even."

"I hear ya," Botts laughed as he headed for the casino floor.

Outside on the Boardwalk there was a line stretching about two blocks. Gamblers waiting for a seat at one of the tables or a spot in front of one of the thousands of shiny slot machines. It had been like that since last spring, when the Renaissance opened.

The first year's drop — the amount of money that crossed the tables and spun through the slots — was in excess of $1 billion. Four times what the experts had originally predicted. Renaissance's profit — its take after taxes, expenses and all the rest — was more than $250 million. For the first nine months of operation, the casino broke all existing industry records. It was doing better than any of the big houses in Las Vegas. Its gross exceeded the take for the entire industry in Reno.

Renaissance Casinos Inc. stock, which you could buy for $2 a share three years ago, was now going for $145.50. And this was after a three-for-one split. A lot of people had made a lot of money already. And this casino gambling thing was just beginning.

Bello didn't get it. This was the only business in the world where people put out cash for a product that was designed to give them no return. The table games were all slanted in the house's favor. The slots were rigged to suck 27 cents out of every dollar. The wheel of fortune was an absolute sucker's bet. Yet people were fighting for spots at the tables. There was a story in the paper the other day about a guy who got arrested for taking a leak in a cup as he sat at a blackjack table. He said he didn't want to give up his seat and go to the men's room because he had waited two hours to get a spot at the table and knew he'd be stuck waiting two more before he could get back at the action.

"Un-fuckin' believable," Bello murmured to himself

as he stepped into one of the revolving doors that quickly spun him out on to the Boardwalk. Across the way, beside the railing that separated the boards from the beach, he saw a silver hot dog vendor's cart shaded by a large and gaudy umbrella. The umbrella was bright red, like Botts' hat. And scrawled in the same fancy yellow lettering were the words "Doggy Man."

"Son of a bitch," thought Bello. "Maybe Nicky has gone legit."

═══

Vinny Barbano had already had his haircut and his facial when Bello walked in. A pretty young girl was doing his nails. Barbano, tanned, silver-haired and stocky, was sitting in a big easy chair in the back of the beauty salon. He held court there every Monday, taking care of business. Networking they call it today.

Tony the Brute, Barbano's driver and bodyguard, stood by the door in the front of the shop looking at the pictures in People Magazine. Bello took the chair next to Barbano. The girl looked at him without smiling. Barbano nodded hello.

Rita Manoff was on the phone arguing, which was like saying she was breathing.

"How many times I gotta tell ya?" she shouted. "I am not IN-TER-EST-ED."

She made a point of slowly enunciating every syllable in the word. Then she slammed down the phone.

"Fortune Realty," she said to the dozen customers and workers who were in her beauty salon. Rita naturally assumed everyone was listening to her conversation. And she wanted them to get the story straight.

"For three months they been pestering me. They want my property, but they don't want to pay my price. They think we're idiots. They're doing the same thing with Angie Marcucci's bakery up the block.

"Hey, we were here first. Now we're supposed to just roll over? Take the first offer and close up shop. Forget it."

Thirty seconds later, Rita came bustling over to where Bello and Barbano were sitting.

"Frankie," she said. "On a Monday? I got you penciled in for Friday. You got a date or what?"

"Rita, one night with you and no other woman can get me excited."

Rita looked at the young woman and then at Vinny Barbano.

"Two weeks ago I asked him for a ride over to St. Michael's for the bingo game. I'm old enough to be ... his big sister."

"A guy can dream, can't he?" Bello said.

"It's been my experience that for most guys, especially guys of a certain age, dreaming is all they can do."

Barbano laughed out loud.

"Beautiful and wise," Bello said with a smile. "What a combination."

"So, you want a trim?"

"Actually, no. I'm here to see Mr. Barbano."

With that, Vinny sat upright in his chair, pulled a roll

of cash out of his pocket and handed the manicurist a
twenty.

"That's all for now, sweetie," he said. "Give us a
minute, will ya?"

The young woman had dark, billowing hair. And
even darker eyes which Bello noticed immediately
because of the look she shot his way. Then she smiled at
Barbano and walked away.

"What's up with her?" Bello asked.

"She's new," said Rita. "And she's serious about her
work. Trust me. It's gonna bother her all day now that
Vinny is walking around with one hand manicured and
one hand not.

"Don't worry. I'll put in a good word for ya."

"Worry?" Bello said. "Why would I worry?"

"Frankie, I know you and pretty girls. I'll take care of
it. You think they all gotta love you."

"No use arguing with her," Vinny Barbano said quietly. "She knows what she knows. Trust me. Now what
can I do for you?"

Rita Manoff had been in the beauty parlor business
for 25 years, which Bello figured put her age at fifty
plus. She had started out in the 1950s doing makeup and
hair backstage at the 500 Club on Mississippi Avenue.
Gave Sinatra a trim one time. He tipped her 50 bucks,
then tried to stick his hand under her blouse.

She threw the money in his face and walked out.

Never looked back.

Vinny Barbano, who was an up-and-comer back

then, heard about it. Liked her right away, even before he met her. Barbano always thought Sinatra was a little bit full of himself. The guy could sing, no question. And he was a poet with a lyric. But that didn't make him no prince.

Barbano bankrolled Rita. She opened up the Casa di Coiffure at Pacific and New York Avenues that summer.

They had their first argument about the name of the place.

"You're mixing tongues here," Vinny said. "Casa is Italian or maybe Spanish. Coiffure (which he pronounced 'quaffer') is what, Canadian? It don't work."

But Rita didn't want to hear. She said it was elegant.

"And besides, we get a lot of vacationers down from Montreal. This way, they feel at home."

"At home, my ass," Vinny said. But he knew he wasn't going to win the argument and so "Casa di Coiffure" it was.

Rita paid Barbano back every penny he put up, thirty grand, which was a lot of money in 1954. Barbano let her slide on the interest. But he took the principal. Put it back on the street as shy money. Before long, he's coming into the shop once a week to get his hair trimmed and to get a facial. He liked to look sharp. And people are stopping in to pay their respects and drop off envelopes. Every Monday like clockwork, Vinny would arrive at 10 a.m. He'd usually stay until noon. And in those two hours he took care of business for the week. People would come to him to settle up on their debts.

They'd pay the vig on the shy money or they'd cover the games they had bet over the weekend.

After the casino opened, manicures became big. The dealers all needed nice-looking fingernails. So Rita put in a manicurist and Barbano added that to his routine.

He never paid for anything, but he always tipped the help. And he always left Rita an envelope. She had a piece of his action. She was making six-for-five. For more than 20 years she had been his partner in the loan shark business. Before the casinos, it was the best game in town.

Now, not so good, but that's getting ahead of the story.

Over the years, people thought she and Vinny had been lovers. But nobody knew for sure. What was certain to anyone who watched them together was that they were friends, good friends. They knew and cared about one another.

When Vinny had his heart attack back in '73, he recuperated in the little apartment Rita kept over the beauty parlor. She had a nice house of her own down on Chelsea Avenue, but she always kept the apartment upstairs open.

People called it their love nest.

She just smiled.

"You never know," she would say.

Rita would cook Vinny chicken soup with escarole and little meatballs, a recipe she learned from her mother, Angelina, who was born in Sicily. Her father, Moe

Manoff, was Jewish. He used to run a little tailor shop on Atlantic Avenue in Ducktown. Angelina and Moe died within a year of each other back in 1964.

"They couldn't live without one another," Rita said. It was one of the few topics she never joked about.

Every night when she was taking care of Vinny, she would feed him her soup and talk about "her people."

"We're full of love and passion," she would say. "But don't cross us. The Jews invented guilt. The Sicilians invented revenge. If provoked, I'll think nothing of naggin' ya to death. So eat your soup."

Barbano, whose parents came from the province of Puglia in southern Italy, loved it.

At first, when he was restricted to his bed, Rita would spoon the soup into his mouth like a baby. She used a large, white napkin to dab at his chin. She knew Vinny was particular about his appearance. She liked that in a man. Later, when he was up and about, they would sit at the small kitchen table, each with a big bowl in front of them.

Rita would talk about her family and Vinny would tell stories about Lecce, the beautiful city in the heel of the Italian peninsula where his mother and father were born.

Rita knew better, but whenever he brought it up, she would ask, "That's where they eat cats, right?"

"No," Vinny would say, feigning anger. "How many times I gotta tell ya. That's Bari, not Lecce. Lecce is the prettiest city in all of Italy. And the thing about it is, nobody knows this. Only the people who live there. Someday I'm gonna go back .... Maybe I'll take you with me."

"We'll see," Rita would say.

Before he moved out of the apartment, Vinny had a big candle-lit dinner sent over from Angelo's Fairmount Tavern. They had Asti Spumante and an antipasto misto and two grilled steaks with broccoli rabe to celebrate his recovery. But Rita insisted that they have some of her soup first.

"The soup is what made you well," she said.

Vinny Barbano loved it. Probably loved her. Although nobody knew for sure. And neither Vinny nor Rita ever talked about it.

Whatever it was, Frankie Bello admired the relationship they had going. Bello was thirty-nine. He had been married once, but that had ended badly more than ten years ago. It had been a long time since he had felt comfortable with a woman.

Bello spent 20 minutes talking with Barbano in the back of the shop. When he left, he kissed Rita on the cheek. The young manicurist, who was working on the hands of a blackjack dealer, never looked up. But Bello was sure he caught her watching him in the mirror as he headed for the door.

Or maybe it was she who caught him.

Chapter 2

Nicky Botts had been involved in a lot of sweet deals in his lifetime, but nothing, absolutely nothing, was as sweet as this scam. Twice a day he walked into the casino with a wad of fives, tens and twenties that added up to $200. Twice a day he headed for the same cashier's booth and, when it was his turn, asked the young girl behind the plastic window for change.

And twice a day he walked out with $20,000. Twenty large. Every day. It was beautiful.

He was on his way to the cage on the morning Frankie Bello spotted him. In fact, while Bello was talking with Barbano, Botts was making another score.

"Gimme 200 ones, will ya hon?" he said as he slid the wad of crumpled bills through the slot in the clear plastic window that separated the gamblers from the money. "I gotta make change. Nobody in this town carries dollar bills no more. Everybody's a freakin' high roller."

The cashier smiled.

"Hot out there today, Mr. Botts?"

"Not too bad," Botts said. "There's a nice breeze off the water. How's business?"

"Couldn't be better," the girl said with a smile.

As they spoke, the girl slid two stacks of bills to the Doggy Man. Each stack was secured with a brown wrapper marked "$100." Botts took the cash, put it in a paper bag and headed back to his spot on the Boardwalk where he'd continue to sell hotdogs. At the end of the day, he'd head back into the casino and cash out another wad. Two trips a day, never any more. One a little before noon and the other a little before 5 p.m. Then he would close up for the day and deliver the cash.

There was $20,000 in each bag.

Forty grand a day, that's what the mob was taking out of the Renaissance Monday through Friday.

Botts didn't work weekends.

It came to two-hundred grand a week, eight-hundred grand a month. They had been working the scam for three months. If they could play it out for an entire year, they'd walk away with $10 million.

They had two girls in the cage, two different shifts. The girls took dollar wrappers meant to wrap around wads of 100 $1 bills, and put them around stacks of $100 bills. Then they slipped a one-dollar bill on the top and on the bottom. Simple. Twice a day like clockwork it went off.

Nicky Botts was, literally, the bag man.

Bello was on the Boardwalk heading back to the Renaissance when the rolling chair pulled up alongside him. It was one of the old-fashioned wicker chairs, the kind you used to see in the pictures from the 1940s Miss America Pageants.

Tommy Sistrunk, his former boss and now the head of security at the Renaissance, was riding in the high-backed seat. He motioned for Bello to get in. The man pushing the chair barely slowed down.

"Frankie, how are things?" Sistrunk said.

"You tell me, Tommy."

"I thought it would be better if we met out here. You keep showing up on the 12th floor and people'll start asking questions. We don't want those jokers from the Division of Gaming Enforcement knocking on your door, do we?"

Bello ignored the question. Already Sistrunk was getting on his nerves.

"You're looking good," Bello said instead, trying to sound like he meant it. "Corporate life agrees with you."

"Can't complain," said Sistrunk. "So, whadda ya think?"

They talked about the case for the next half hour as the chair rolled up and down the Boardwalk. Actually, Sistrunk did most of the talking. He asked a lot of questions, pumping Bello for theories and possiblities. But he offered very little in return. What else is new, Bello thought. The guy never changes.

"How about the maintenance guy who found the stuff?" Bello asked.

"No way he's involved," said Sistrunk. "We checked him up and down."

"Still, I'd like to talk with him," Bello said.

"No can do."

"Oh?"

"He don't live here no more. He's been transferred. He's heading up a maintenance crew at our casino in the Bahamas. Mr. Bradley decided he was supervisory material."

"Just like that."

"It's like I always told ya, Frankie, knowledge is power. You gotta go along to get along. But you were always too hard headed. Always had to do 'the right thing.' Where'd it get ya?

"Here's a guy finds a gym bag and parlays it into a $50,000-a-year job in the Bahamas. Plus he's got a rent-free house on the beach just outside of Nassau and a company car. A Volvo, I think. Tell me where else that could happen."

"It's the American dream," Bello said. "Guy works hard all his life, deserves something like that."

"Absolutely," said Sistrunk.

"I suppose he's signed a confidentiality agreement."

"Suppose all you want," said Sistrunk.

"I'm guessing his promotion, new house, car, all of that is contingent on him never mentioning the gym bag to anyone."

"I think," said Sistrunk, "that if you were able to ask Mr. Alvarez, he would say, 'What gym bag?'"

"So where's that leave us?"

Sistrunk said his "intelligence" indicated that there were several possible sources for "the problem."

"It might be the wiseguys from New York making a move, although I don't think so. It could be we got some half-assed hustler, some wannabe wiseguy, freelancing, which is why I wanted you in this case. Nobody moves in those circles better than you."

Sistrunk paused.

"Or?" Bello said.

"Or it could be that we've got an international situation."

"International?"

"Yeah. You read the papers. Did you see where the Shah went when he left Iran?"

It had been in the news for weeks late last year. The Shah was forced out by Islamic fundamentalists. Fled at night with an entourage of sycophants and several hundred million dollars. Ended up in the penthouse of the Renaissance Regal Casino Hotel in the Bahamas. Funny, Bello thought, Tonio Alvarez might be sweeping up after him right now.

"We think this might be coming from Tehran," Sistrunk said solemnly. "I was talking with a friend of mine in Washington."

"And?"

"A lot of this comes to me on a need-to-know basis,"

said Sistrunk, acting now more like the FBI agent he always wished he had been rather than the precinct captain that he used to be. "And quite frankly, you don't need to know."

Sistrunk paused to let that sink in.

"I want you to work the wiseguy angle," Sistrunk said finally.

Bello had forgotten how much Tommy enjoyed giving orders.

"Once we've confirmed the source of the problem we'll set our parameters. Maybe we won't need ya. For now we move on parallel lines. The call comes in tonight at 7. Use the service entrance and come up the back elevator. I'll have somebody waiting on the 12th floor to bring you to the office."

Bello looked up at the clear blue sky. A warm salt breeze was blowing off the ocean, an early taste of Spring. He wished he were working some divorce case, or an insurance claim. At least you knew what and who you were dealing with. He was starting to get a headache.

The wicker chair continued up the Boardwalk toward the Renaissance. Sistrunk was talking about the old days in the police department. Bello thought about jumping off and walking away. "Do I fuckin' need this aggravation?" he asked himself. Then he thought of the paycheck and decided to ride it out for awhile, at least until the phone call.

That was his plan. Then they heard the explosion.

"What the hell was that?" said Sistrunk.

Bello looked up. From behind the tops of the buildings that lined the Boardwalk — the James Salt Water Taffy Store, the Wild West leather goods shop, the Three Brothers Pizzeria — a plume of black smoke was shooting toward the sky.

Bello and Sistrunk both jumped from the rolling chair and began to run toward the ramp that led to New York Avenue. Half the tourists on the Boardwalk seemed to be moving in that direction. By the time Bello reached the bottom of the ramp he had been separated from Sistrunk. He was sandwiched in a crowd of several hundred people, all craning to see what had happened. The crowd pushed forward toward the smoke. Sirens were wailing. The street was crammed with fire trucks, police cruisers and an ambulance.

By the time Bello reached the scene, the cops had already cordoned off a parking lot with yellow crime scene tape. Three fire hoses were spraying water on the heap of a Lincoln Continental which was still very much engulfed in flames.

Bello recognized the car immediately.

It was Vinny Barbano's.

Chapter 3

F or three months Nick Botts dropped the money off like clockwork. Every afternoon, between 5:30 and 6 p.m., he showed up at the construction company office on Georgia Avenue.

But on the day Vinny Barbano got blown away, Botts was told not to come by. And that's what started all the trouble.

Nicky Botts was a degenerate gambler. Had been all his life. Cards. Dice. Horses. Football. Forgetaboutit. Nicky Botts' idea of heaven was bettin'.

And broads.

Usually in that order.

He was 48 years old and had wrecked three marriages while gambling away, by his own estimation, close to a half-million dollars. He couldn't help himself. It wasn't even a conscious act. To Nicky Botts, betting was like waking up in the morning. He would stop when he was dead.

For more than 20 years he had been what the feds

called a "mob associate." This meant that he wasn't a "made" guy, but that he was "with" made guys.

Associates were usually money-makers and Botts fit the bill perfectly. He was a master con man. He could talk himself into or out of anything. There wasn't a scam he hadn't pulled. There were several, in fact, that he had invented. But if he made a score on a Wednesday, he was usually broke by Sunday morning.

Blame it on geography.

On Thursday nights there was always a big monte game at the South Philadelphia War Veterans Club — members and guests only. Botts was a regular, even though he had washed out of the National Guard after three months. Something about a stolen shipment of canned goods that found its way from the National Guard Armory to a flea market run by Botts' cousin Tony.

Now if Botts came out of the monte game flush, there were poker, craps and zignetti games in the back-rooms of a half dozen mob clubhouses downtown, some of which ran all weekend. Botts might roll in with a wad of cash, but he usually ended up borrowing money for car fare home.

Then he'd be out all week looking for his next score. And if he hit, he'd head for the monte game. It was one continuous cycle.

It was only natural that Botts ended up in Atlantic City when the first casino opened. He was "on loan" to the Little Guy, Paolo "Little Paulie" Scarpino.

Scarpino was an ex-prize fighter with a mean streak. He had been a hitter for Barbano, although the two mobsters could barely tolerate one another. Barbano thought Scarpino was too much of a show-off. Scarpino thought Barbano was too set in his ways, too much "old school, mustache Pete bullshit," he would say.

Scarpino was always looking for the big score. He was out there grabbing with both fists, using fear and intimidation to horn his way into everybody's action. Barbano was more laissez-faire. He took the long view. Plan your work and work your plan, he would say. Let everybody earn. Be patient.

"We all wanna make money," Vinny said when he was still trying to talk sense into Scarpino. "What we don't wanna make is headlines. Capesce?"

But Scarpino never really understood.

He was a tough guy and wanted everybody to know it. What's more, he wanted everybody to pay tribute. Scarpino first locked horns with Barbano over the street tax. Scarpino wanted a piece of everyone's action. He started demanding that anyone taking bets or loaning money pay him a percentage of what they were making.

Barbano went nuts. It was no way to do business, he said.

One of the first bookmakers Scarpino hit on was Vinny's uncle, Salvatore Rosato. He ran a candy store on Florida Avenue just off the Boardwalk. He had a little book on the side. During the football season he might earn $200 a week. It was penny ante stuff. Scarpino wanted a piece. He didn't know Rosato was related to Vinny. He sent two guys around and they threatened the old man.

Sal Rosato called his nephew Vinny to complain.

"I'll take care of it, Uncle Sal," Vinny said. Then he told his uncle to arrange a second meeting with Scarpino's two goons.

Barbano and Tony the Brute were waiting when they arrived.

"Uncle Sal, go take a walk on the boards," Vinny said.

Then Barbano and the Brute tuned up Scarpino's two wiseguys. They ended up in the emergency room of the Atlantic City Medical Center.

Scarpino got the message. That was the end of the street tax. Barbano had exerted his authority. Scarpino backed off. But it was just a matter of time before the two went at it again.

It was personal.

They hated each other's guts.

With the opening of the first casino, the rift between the two widened. Botts heard that Scarpino was traveling up to New York on a regular basis. The word was he was lining up support from one of the big families up there so that he could make a move on Vinny.

That's what Botts figured had gone down when he heard about the car bombing that took out Barbano.

The call came in over the pay phone located on the Boardwalk next to his hot dog vendor's cart.

Two rings. Then silence. Then two rings again. And silence. That was the signal.

When the phone rang a third time, Nicky Botts picked up.

"Yeah?"

"You heard?

"You kiddin'? The whole Boardwalk's buzzing."

"Okay. Don't come around today. We're closing up early. Too much heat. The Eye-balls have been around already. Hold on to everything until tomorrow."

"Eye-balls" meant FBI. That's the way Scarpino and his crew talked. "Freakin' Eye-balls," they would say. Or sometimes it would be "the three initials."

Subtlety wasn't one of Scarpino's strong points. Neither, it would turn, was intelligence. But that's getting ahead of the story.

"I hear ya," Botts said. Then he hung up the phone.

An hour later, Botts was in line at the cashier's cage making "change" for a wad of fives, tens and twenties. Once again the girl behind the plastic window passed out two of the special stacks, each with 100 $100 bills covered in wrappers marked "$100. "Botts put the money in a brown paper bag, just as he did every afternoon.

But since he didn't have to rush over to Scarpino's construction company office to drop off the bags, he stopped in the casino lounge and ordered a Rolling Rock. This, he would realize later, was not a good move. By the third beer he was feeling lucky. His right hand was itching. And the two bags of cash, which he had wedged between his thighs on the bar stool, were pressing against his crotch like a lap dancer looking for a big tip.

Botts started out at the craps table with $1,000 worth of chips. In his mind, he called this an advance. Scarpino was paying him a grand a week for working the scam.

Botts knew he should have been getting more. They were taking $200,000 out of the casino each week. But he was in no position to complain. He had no leverage.

When he left Philly to come down the Shore, Botts owed Louie the Lip $30,000. He had to come up with $600 a week just to cover the vig. Forget about paying down the principal. Scarpino assumed that debt from The Lip and told Botts that he was taking a piece of the scam each week to cover the loan.

Still, Botts figured he was being cheated.

He had come up with the idea for scamming the casino. He made the contact with the two broads who worked in the cashier's cage. He was the one who had wined and dined them, persuaded them to go along. Scarpino was sending them each $500 a week. Not a lot of money, but they were kids and were excited just to be around gangsters.

That's how it went. People, all kinds of people, loved being around wiseguys. It made them feel special.

So now Botts is at the craps table playing with his grand, the mental advance he has given himself on his pay. In 10 minutes he runs that up to $2,200 and orders his first vodka tonic. When the leggy cocktail waitress brings him his drink, he puts a fifty-dollar chip on her tray.

"Don't forget about me hon," he says. "I plan to play awhile."

"Awhile" turned out to be four hours.

It wasn't pretty.

It was one of the darkest and longest runs of bad luck in the young history of casino gambling in Atlantic City.

First craps.

Then blackjack.

By 10 p.m. Nicky Botts had lost $39,250 of Paulie Scarpino's money.

Needless to say, he did not show up for work the next day. Or the day after that.

By Wednesday afternoon, Scarpino had somebody else selling hot dogs and cashing out at the casino. And by Thursday, the night of Vinny Barbano's wake, Scarpino had people all over the city looking for Botts.

"I want him here," Scarpino said. "I want him here now. Bring him whole or bring him in pieces. It don't matter."

Chapter 4

Vinny Barbano was laid out in style.

The viewing took place at D'Alfonso's Funeral Home on Atlantic Avenue. This was just around the corner from St. Michael's Church where, following several phone calls and much theological debate, it was decided that the monsignor would celebrate a Funeral Mass for Vincenzo Salvatore Barbano, a fine and upstanding child of the church who may or may not have been "the alleged mob boss" of Atlantic City.

"To the Romans, Christ was an alleged revolutionary," the monsignor had said to the bishop's representative, a pasty-faced young priest who had raised some initial objections to the funeral arrangements. "We have no idea what was in this man's heart when he died. I'm saying the Mass."

The bishop — after learning of the donations Barbano had made to the diocese over the years and after Barbano's lawyer, Bernie Kestlebaum, informed him that an even larger bequest was part of Barbano's will — softened his objections. With that, the young priest quickly dropped his opposition. In fact, he insisted on concelebrating.

But first there was the viewing.

More than 500 people lined up along Atlantic Avenue at 7 p.m. when Domenic D'Alfonso opened the ornate doors. As they filed in, D'Alfonso handed each mourner a holy card with a picture of the Blessed Virgin and asked each to sign his or her name in the visitors' book perched on the podium by the doorway leading to the room where the casket was located. The place was awash in flowers, all kinds of bouquets, each with a different salutation. There were "Uncle Vinny," "Vincenzo," "Amico Mio" and "Cara Mia." There was also a flower spray designed like a clock with the hands set at 12:35, the time the bomb went off.

Frankie Bello stood in line for over an hour, ending up right behind a city councilman and the city solicitor, both of whom were on Vinny's pad.

The private eye heard snippets of conversation, but his mind kept drifting in and out of the present. He had been working the Renaissance extortion case for three days and was hung up on the timing.

A bomb and a threatening letter are planted in the baccarat pit of the casino hotel Monday morning. That afternoon another bomb blows Vinny Barbano away.

Bello's gut told him there was a connection. But for three days all he had been doing was running into brick walls. He decided to take a few hours off and pay his respects to Barbano. He wished he had had a chance to talk with the mob boss one more time. Their last conversation had been full of questions but short on answers.

Across the street, the feds were set up in a van. They made no attempt to hide what they were up to. An FBI agent in a dark suit, white shirt and striped tie was sitting in the passenger seat pointing a camera and snapping away at those who had come to say goodbye to Vinny Barbano.

"Is that necessary?" asked the councilman, who made a point of facing away from the camera. "Is there no respect anymore? Can't they leave the man in peace?"

In front of the councilman were two middle-aged couples who were talking in hushed tones about "the bombing."

"He never knew what hit him," said one man, acting as if he knew more than he was able to say. "That's the only good thing. He went quick."

"But what a shame for his family," said a brassy blonde who was on the arm of the guy who knew it all. "A closed casket. His family can't say a proper goodbye. It's so sad. I feel so bad for them."

Behind Bello were two older men with their wives, retirees whom Bello saw occasionally when he dropped Rita Manoff at the bingo game at the church hall.

"He may be dead," one of the old men said to the other, making the sign of the cross as he did so, "but you don't know the problems I got."

"Don't start," said one of the older women, obviously his wife.

Then to the other woman, "This one lives to complain. All day, every day."

Then to the husband.

"You should just thank God you can complain. Look at Vinny. Who can he complain to?"

"Some day, and that day may be soon, I'll be gone. And then you'll wish you could hear me complain."

"Some day you'll be gone and I'll finally get some rest."

The banter made Bello think of Rita and Vinny and how they used to joke and tease one another at the beauty parlor. Now Vinny was gone. And Rita was inside, dressed in black, saying goodbye to the only man she had ever loved.

━━━━

The police had questioned Bello twice about the car-bombing death of Vinny Barbano. Mostly, they wanted to know what Bello and Barbano had talked about that morning at the beauty parlor.

"You're probably one of the last people to talk with him," Detective Mike Quincy had said. "Anything you'd like to share with us?"

"Not really," Bello said. "I'm working on a case. I thought Mr. Barbano might be able to help me out."

"Did he?"

"Not really."

Quincy wasn't a bad guy, but he was clearly frustrated. This was the biggest mob hit in the history of the city. Vinny Barbano had been the boss of Atlantic City for nearly 10 years. He'd never spent a day in jail and in several neighborhoods he was more popular than the mayor. Could have been the mayor, in fact. Quincy knew he had to act quickly. The longer the case dragged on, the more likely the feds — the Eyeballs — would come in and take it over.

"Quince, if I had anything I thought would help ya, I'd give it up," Bello had said. "But I just got nothing for ya."

That was on Monday afternoon, a few hours after the murder.

Two days later, Bello was called down to the police administration building for a second interview. They covered the same ground and again Bello offered nothing. This time, Quincy had more to go on. He told Bello some of the details forensics had picked up. Three sticks of dynamite had been rigged behind the dashboard of Barbano's Lincoln.

"Looks like they used some half-assed remote control device."

Bello thought of the gym bag and the dynamite spread out on the coffee table in the executive suite of the Renaissance casino hotel Monday morning. The extortionist hadn't rigged the dynamite to the timer, but the bag included a cheap remote control device, the kind you could pick up at a Radio Shack for $12.95.

In fact, Bello had priced the item. There were seven electronics stores in the immediate Atlantic City area. They all carried the devices. And they all sold them on a regular basis. They were compatible with all kinds of kids' toys.

"It's a real popular item," a clerk at a store on the Boardwalk had told Bello. "We can't keep them in stock."

Bello had no intention of sharing any of this with Quincy, but he was happy to let the detective talk.

"Barbano was barbecue," Quincy said. "Un-fuckin'-believable. We made the ID through a partial dental plate we found on the back seat. I was at the morgue. What a mess."

Quincy reached into the top drawer of his desk and pulled out a bottle of Excedrin. He twisted off the lid and shook three tablets into the palm of his hand. Then he quickly slipped them into his mouth and reached for the cup of coffee on his desk to wash them down.

"It never stops," he said. "My plate was already full when Barbano got blown away. Now the mayor's callin' all the time for a status report. He's got Time Magazine and the New York Times calling about a 'mob war in casino city' and he wants some answers. On top of that, they got me working with the arson investigators from the Fire Department. We had two more fires last night, an apartment building and a vacant store. Both in the

Inlet. And I'll bet next week's pay when we run the check, these properties will belong to Fortune Realty. They're out there playing Monopoly. Buying up property and looking to cash in when a casino developer comes along."

Bello recognized the name. Rita Manoff had taken a call from the company at the beauty parlor. The salesman wanted to buy her place.

"They buy apartments, stores, restaurants, whatever," Quincy said. "But they don't want the business income or the rent. They want the land. So they burn the places down. That way no headaches. No problems collecting rent. No complaints about heaters that don't work or toilets that don't flush.

"Plus they collect the insurance. What a scam. Sometimes I think this whole city is one big hustle."

"I like it," said Bello. "Call the Chamber of Commerce."

Quincy fell right in with the patter.

"You could put it on the billboards out along the Expressway and the Black Horse Pike. Forget New York, the Big Apple. Who needs New Orleans, the Big Easy? Come to Atlantic City, the Big Hustle."

Midway through the interview, a uniform stuck his head in the door.

"Mike, I got that custodian on the phone."

"Tell him we're sending a car over this afternoon," Qunicy said.

Then he looked at Bello.

"You won't believe this one. That's the morgue. They should call it the zoo. The mayor's got six no-show jobs down there, family members of all his ward leaders. All kinds of supplies are walking out the back door. Nobody knows where anything is. Today we get this call about a missing body. The sergeant's taking the information. 'When did this happen, sir?' He goes, 'I'm not sure. Sometime Sunday night.' The sergeant goes, 'Sir, this is Wednesday. Is there some reason why you waited so long to call us?' And this guy, what a schmuck. What's the word in Italian?"

"*Chiadrule*," Bello said.

"Yeah, this *chiadrule*, he goes, 'Well, I was hoping it might turn up.' Like maybe he filed it in the wrong drawer or something. A freakin' corpse. You oughta be happy you're out of this line of work, Frankie. It ain't gettin' any better."

━━━━━━

Rita Manoff was seated in the second row facing the casket. Frankie Bello, after paying his respects to Barbano's family members, slid into the seat next to her. He kissed her on the cheek. Gave her a hug. The manicurist was sitting on Rita's left. Both women wore black dresses, dark stockings and hardly any make-up. The young woman was even better looking than Bello had thought when he first saw her in the beauty parlor.

Rita's eyes were rubbed raw from crying but she smiled and took Frankie's hand. She held it tight without saying anything.

Barbano's three sisters and a slew of nieces, nephews and cousins filled the first row. Everyone lined up to talk with them, but anybody who really knew Vinny stopped to talk with Rita as well.

Rita introduced the young woman to Bello.

"Frankie, this is my cousin Sammy's daughter, Julia," she said. "I know you two ran into each other the other day... ."

Bello held out his hand.

Julia shook it politely. Then she put her arm on Rita's shoulder.

"He was a good man," Frankie said.

"You don't know how good," Rita said. "There are people in this room who don't know yet how much they're going to miss him."

As she was saying that, Bello saw Paulie Scarpino making his way to the front of the casket.

He wore a gray suit, hand-tailored, with a white shirt and a white tie. He had a Rolex watch on his left wrist, which he made a point of flashing on a regular basis, and a diamond pinky ring on his right hand. Two young goons stood behind him. Bello recognized them as the Prato brothers, Matteo and Marco. They had gone to work for Scarpino shortly after Vinny and Tony the Brute sent Scarpino's other two henchmen to the hospital. Matty Prato held Scarpino's topcoat. Black. Cashmere. Marc Prato surveyed the room.

Scarpino made a great show of kneeling down in front of the casket, blessing himself and burying his head in his hands, as if in prayer.

"*Animale*," Rita Manoff hissed quietly in Sicilian.

"*Goniff*," she added just as vehemently in Yiddish.

━━━

Two hours later, Bello was sitting at the bar in the Town Tavern on the corner of Texas and Pacific Avenues a block off the Boardwalk nursing a Frangelico over ice. Rita Manoff sat next to him working on her second gin-and-tonic. Julia had a coke.

"Nothing stronger?" Bello asked.

"Not tonight," she said. "Maybe some other time."

Bello liked the possibility in her answer.

"You know, Frankie, Vinny always liked you," Rita said.

"And I liked him," Bello said.

"He told me he was sorry he couldn't help you with whatever it was you came to see him about that day."

"It was a long-shot."

"How's that going?"

Bello sipped his drink. He looked in the mirror behind the bar and saw Rita's reflection. She looked empty. There was no other way to describe her. She had aged 10 years in four days. Her eyes, which were usually alive and dancing, were blank and lifeless.

Bello thought about how sad it all was.

And wondered if anyone would ever love him as much as she had loved Vinny.

Even though Rita asked the question, she didn't

seem to be interested in the answer. Julia toyed with a napkin and appeared to be lost in her own thoughts.

"It's going," Bello said. "I'll know more Saturday night."

———

The extortionist had called the Renaissance at 7 p.m. Monday, just as the note had said. The conversation, which Tom Sistrunk had recorded, lasted all of ninety seconds. Short and to the point, the message laid out the plan for payment.

It was bold and brilliant.

Whoever was behind this had a sense of style, Bello thought.

And timing.

G. Malcolm Bradley was not amused. This was only going to cause more problems. It was bad enough that he had kept the Division of Gaming Enforcement in the dark about the bomb threat. Bradley could justify that in his mind and was sure the board of directors would understand. A bomb in a casino was bad for business, no question. Even worse would be the rumor of a bomb.

Resorts International, the Renaissance Corp.'s main competitor in the Bahamas, was scheduled to open a casino on the Boardwalk in a week. Both Bally's and Caesars World hoped to be up and running by the end of the summer.

If the threat of a bomb scared gamblers away, they might never come back. Especially if other, newer places were available.

No, Bradley knew he was right keeping the bomb threat quiet.

But the payoff was more problematic.

Now he would have to rig a baccarat game.

That was how and where the payoff was to take place.

Saturday night at the baccarat table. The same table where Antonio Alvarez had found the gym bag. A "representative," that's the term the extortionist used, would show up at 8 p.m. and begin gambling at the $100-minimum table.

By midnight, the extortionist said, the representative would cash in his chips. At that point, he should have $4 million in front of him.

"You can make it happen," the extortionist had said quietly and confidently. "Or we can make you sorry."

If that ever got out, there would be no way for Bradley to protect himself. Not even the chief executive officer of the city's first and only casino could weather that storm. The state would yank his license in a minute. Probably close the casino as well. He could even be indicted.

"Who is this son of a bitch?" Bradley said.

"We're working on it," Sistrunk said, a little too quickly.

"Well you're not working hard enough," Bradley said, his neck turning red under the white, highly starched collar of his $85 Kenneth Cole dress shirt.

Bello sat quietly in his chair, watching Sistrunk and Bradley, trying to figure which one, the casino head of security or the CEO, he liked least.

It was a toss-up.

"I wouldn't be surprised if our friends down the Boardwalk are behind this," Bradley said.

"No way," said Sistrunk. "They got to be licensed, too. Something liked this backed up on them, they'd never be able to open their casinos. The state would run them out of town. This is an outside job. I'm sure of that."

"What do you think, Mr. Bello?"

Bradley was trying to draw him into the conversation, something Bello hoped to avoid. He waited a few seconds before replying.

"It's brilliant," he said finally. "So I'd have to agree with Tommy. Nobody in the casino industry would have the balls to come up with something like this."

Two days after the Monday night phone call, Bradley got a note in the mail — local postmark, no other identifiers — that provided the number of a Swiss bank account. The caller had said that after his "representative" cashed out, the money, less the necessary taxes, should be wired abroad.

"Brilliant," Bello said again. "They're even gonna pay their taxes."

Bradley failed to see the humor in it all.

But Bello didn't care. There was something else going on here that neither Bradley nor Sistrunk was willing to share with him. Bello knew he wasn't get the whole story.

His instincts told him that the extortion of the casino was somehow connected to the bomb blast that blew away mob boss Vinny Barbano.

And whether they liked it or not, Bello intended to find out how.

Chapter 5

The red light was blinking on the answering machine when Frankie Bello entered his apartment.

It was a little after midnight.

Bello had been gone all day. He had worked the extortion investigation, then gone to Vinny Barbano's wake. From the wake, he took Rita and Julia to the Town Tavern for a drink. After walking the two women home, he hopped a jitney to Ventnor. That time of night it was a 10-minute ride. The Jitney stop was three doors from his apartment, a second-floor walkup on Atlantic Avenue, two blocks from the Boardwalk. The place had a large living room with a fake fireplace, a bedroom, a bath and a small galley kitchen. Bello ate out most days, so that was more than enough. The rent was $650 a month.

Not a bad deal.

He also used the place as his office. The answering machine was his secretary. Now the red light was blinking steadily. Three calls.

Bello started to peel off his shirt as he hit the play button.

"Frankie! Frankie! It's me, Botts. I needa talk to ya. Pick up."

The second message was more of the same.

"Yo, Frankie, where the hell are ya? Pick up. Pick up."

And finally, even more urgently.

"Frankie, I got nowhere else to turn. Where are you? All right. Listen to me. I can't call no more tonight. If you get this, meet me on the Boardwalk in front of the place tomorrow morning. You know, the swag place. Make it around 10:30. I'll find you. Just be there."

Bello had been wondering about Botts for the last two days.

Mike Quincy had asked about him during the second interview at the police station. The cops were looking for Botts and Tony the Brute, Vinny Barbano's bodyguard. Both had turned up missing after Vinny got hit.

"We figure they'll show up eventually," Quincy had said. "Either in the trunk of a car or at low tide. Ain't many places you can hide a body on this island."

The cops were working on the theory that Barbano was taken out in a power play. Quincy had it figured one of two ways: either "Little Paulie" Scarpino was flexing his muscle or the boys from New York were making a move.

But Bello wasn't so sure. He didn't think Scarpino had the guts or the moxie to make a move on Barbano. And he knew the last thing the wiseguys in New York wanted at this point was a mob war. Casino gambling was just beginning. For months, conservative politicians and church groups that had opposed the gambling referendum had been warning that legalized gaming would bring organized crime to the city.

Bello had to laugh when he heard that argument. The mob had been in the city for years. Barbano was a freakin' fixture, for crying out loud. But the point was that a high profile mob killing — and blowing up Vinny Barbano and his Lincoln Continental in broad daylight a block from the Boardwalk was nothing if not high profile — would only add fuel to the simmering fire that was the anti-casino movement.

The mob guys from New York wanted to make money, not headlines. They were on the same page as Barbano when it came to the opportunities that casino gambling presented.

And while Scarpino was not sophisticated enough to appreciate the concept of a slow, patient, long-term corruption of the industry, neither was he arrogant enough to think he could take on both New York and Barbano.

So while the cops were looking for the mob behind the Barbano hit, Bello sensed there was something else, some other type of play.

He agreed with Quincy, however, when the detective speculated that whoever had killed Barbano would take out Tony the Brute as well.

If The Brute had betrayed Barbano and set him up, then whoever used him would eliminate him just to clean up loose ends. If he was loyal to his boss — and everything Bello knew about The Brute indicated he was — then he was dead. If not, he would be a problem for Vinny's killers.

Botts was another matter. Bello didn't know where he fit in the picture. And Quincy wasn't offering much, except to say that Nicky hadn't been seen for three days and that Scarpino was turning the city upside-down looking for him.

Botts was part of Scarpino's crew, but he wasn't a hitter. As far as the cops or the feds knew, Botts was not into violence. He could talk you to death, but he didn't go in for guns or knives or bombs.

Bello, who was eight years younger, had known Botts since he was a kid. Their parents were neighbors in South Philly, on Iseminger Street, near 13th and Wharton. When he was 12, Bello had moved with his mother and father to Atlantic City. By the time Bello joined the Police Department 10 years later, Botts was just a boyhood memory.

But Bello's mother used to speak fondly of him.

"He was such a cute little boy," she would say. "It's a shame. Growing up without a father. His father was away, you know."

"Ma, I know," Frankie would say. "He was a bank robber."

Nicky's father was doing 30 years at Eastern State. So Nicky Botts was raised by his mother and his maternal grandfather. The mother wasn't around too much, though, so the old man was all he had.

"That's how he got the nickname," Bello's mother said. And then she would tell the story. Bello's mom loved to talk about the old days in South Philadelphia. And Frankie Bello, good son that he was, loved to listen.

"Poppa George — that's what everybody called Nicky's grandfather — used to take the boy over to the playground around Ninth and Wharton. Back in them days there was a bocce ball court in the corner of the park.

"Some of the older men would play every day, spring through fall. Nicky would tag along. He was, what, five or six years old. And the old men, they would always get into arguments. In Italian. And somebody would always say to somebody else, 'You're crazy.'

"Only they would say it in that heavy, Sicilian dialect where t's sound like d's and p's sound like b's. Anyway, they would holler at one another, '*Tu sei pazzo!*' You know, 'You're crazy.'

"But little Nicky, what he would hear was 'doozie botts.' So one day his grandfather's giving him a lecture 'cause he had done something wrong, caused some kind of problem, and the little boy starts hollering, just like he hears at the bocce court.

'Doozie botts. Doozie botts.'

"It takes the old man a second to realize what the kid is saying, then he breaks up laughing. Now he's going up and down the street, making Little Nicky tell everyone. 'Doozie botts.'

"After that, whenever Nicky Carlucci was walking

down the street, people would holler, 'Yo, Botts.' Or, 'Hey, Nicky Botts.' So that's where the nickname came from.

"It's wrong, what they put in the paper. Makes it sound like he's a criminal just because he's got a nickname."

"But Ma, he is a criminal," Frankie Bello would say.

"Still, it's a shame," Bello's mother would say. "He was such a nice little boy. Doozie botts."

When Botts showed up in Atlantic City several years later, Bello made a point of re-establishing a connection. Before long Botts became a source, passing on information that Bello, who was then a city police detective, was able to use. Botts was a master manipulator. Knew how to play the game. Would give up just enough information to keep you interested, but not enough to jam himself up or, even worse, put himself in jeopardy of being subpoenaed to testify before a grand jury or at a trial.

"I'm strictly a CI, right, Frankie?" Botts would say. "Confidential informant. Emphasis on confidential. This is just between you and me. I got your word, right?"

"My word and my 50 bucks," Bello would say, handing over the cash. "What have you got for me?"

Botts had once helped Bello build a case against a stolen property ring that was ripping off construction sites in the city. He also gave up some pretty good information on a gang of low-level cocaine dealers that eventually led to a bigger case against a couple of suppliers. True to his word, Bello never disclosed where his info was coming from and Botts never had to testify.

When Bello left the police department a year ago he lost touch with Botts. Then he bumped into him that morning outside the Renaissance.

Now this.

How did Botts fit into the Barbano hit, Bello wondered? More important, why was he calling him?

They used to meet on the Boardwalk in front of a store called Castle of Bargains. It was a gaudy discount store stocked with over-priced china, silverware, pottery and jewelry. Bello figured half the stuff had fallen off the back of a truck. In fact, Botts was probably a major supplier. He dealt in swag on a regular basis. Bello never doubted that the stolen property ring Botts helped him finger was his competition. This made being a good citizen a profitable enterprise on several different levels. It was a classic Botts move.

Bello was up and out of his apartment by nine the next morning. He walked the boards to the meeting place, arriving there a little before ten. The sun was gleaming off the ocean. White caps were breaking. It was a glorious day, the kind of day that made all the other aggravation of the week dissolve, at least momentarily. All the honky tonk and all the casino glitz and glitter paled next to a morning with the sun coming up over the ocean, the breeze blowing cool and steady in off the water and the seagulls chattering in the background.

Bello turned around. The Boardwalk was already crowded. A parade of people was headed toward the Renaissance which was opening for another day of business.

Mister Peanut was standing in front of Castle of Bargains waving and handing out free samples.

Bello remembered Mister Peanut from when he was a kid. The character was a piece of the old Atlantic City, a Muppet long before Big Bird and the rest of them started showing up on public television.

Mister Peanut would stand out on the Boardwalk for hours every day in front of the old Planter's Peanut Store, waving to the tourists and handing out free, but very small, bags of roasted nuts to the kids. There were probably four peanuts in the bag, two of which might have been edible.

Still, people loved him.

So when Planter's closed its store, Castle of Bargains grabbed the franchise. There was now a roasted nuts section sandwiched in between the china and the jewelry.

Typical Atlantic City.

Mister Peanut wore black tuxedo pants. The top half of his body was a huge peanut shell. Eyes, nose and mouth were painted on the front of the shell and a large, black top hat, set at a rakish angle, rested atop the body. The character stood about seven feet tall and on good days, when the Boardwalk was jumping, kids swarmed all over him.

To many people, Mister Peanut was a reminder of the way things used to be. The Steel Pier and the diving horse were gone; so were the Italian Village and the Million Dollar Pier. Most of the movie theaters, the Strand, the Warner, the Apollo, the Lyric, had closed

years earlier. Salt Water Taffy and Mister Peanut were all that were left of the old, pre-casino Boardwalk.

Bello had a cup of coffe from the Dunkin' Donuts. He was sipping slowly, leaning up against the railing that separated the Boardwalk from the beach, watching the ocean, lost in his reverie. Then he heard someone whisper, "Yo, Frankie."

It was Mister Peanut. He had sauntered over from in front of the store and was now standing next to Bello, leaning on the railing, staring out at the ocean trying to act nonchalant, as if that were a normal thing for a seven-foot puppet to be doing.

"Botts, is that you?" Bello said.

"Who the hell else would it be? I'm dying in here. I just wanted to make sure you were OK. I been watching ya for 20 minutes, making sure you weren't followed."

"Thanks for the vote of confidence."

"Frankie, not for nuthin', but you don't know what I been through. Meet me inside, the storage room in the back. Five minutes."

Just then two little girls came running up.

"Mister Peanut! Mister Peanut!"

Botts threw them each four bags of peanuts. Flung them, actually, out onto the Boardwalk the way some people fling birdseed at the pigeons. The girls scrambled after the goodies.

"Freakin' kids gimme a headache," Botts muttered.

Then, to Bello, "Five minutes. We gotta talk."

Chapter 6

Tommy Sistrunk, the head of security for the Renaissance Casino Hotel, was standing in the bow of the Regal II, a forty-foot luxury yacht that was at the constant disposal of G. Malcolm Bradley, the casino's CEO.

The ex-cop thought he had seen it all. But what was playing out in front of him would be hard to top. Thank God they were 30 miles out, somewhere off the coast of Sea Isle City.

There were a half-dozen federal and state law enforcement agencies who would die for a photograph of what Sistrunk was watching.

There, sitting across a small table from each other on the highly polished wooden deck of the Regal II was Bradley, the top casino executive in the city, and Paolo "Little Paulie" Scarpino.

Scarpino was seething.

Sistrunk could see the back of his thick neck turning red.

"It's out of control," Scarpino said. "This is not the

way it was supposed to go down."

"I understand and agree," Bradley said calmly. "But we have to be able to make adjustments.

Scarpino's 25-foot sport fishing boat, the *Amica Nostra,* was bobbing on the water about fifty feet away. He and his son, Paulie Jr., had taken a skiff over to the large yacht.

Paulie Jr. was standing off to the side, behind his father. He was part of the meeting, but was not invited to the table. Neither was Sistrunk.

Bradley wanted it that way.

Sistrunk had piloted the yacht. No one else was on board.

"Highest security," Bradley had told him when he set up the trip. That meant he and Sistrunk would be traveling alone.

On the boat ride out from the Atlantic City Marina, Bradley had discussed the problem with Sistrunk. Sistrunk realized this made him part of a conspiracy, but he was more than willing to go along.

His salary, $250,000 a year, and the perks that came with the job, a free hotel room, showgirls, unlimited drinks and meals, more than made up for any qualms of conscience the former cop may have had.

"Someone, obviously, thinks they can take advantage of the situation," Bradley told Sistrunk after they had headed out from the marina. "I intend to find out who."

The bomb threat had come in Monday morning, four

days earlier. The payoff was due on Saturday. Bradley said that before he paid anyone $4 million he wanted to know two things, who he was paying and what guarantee did he have that he would not have to pay again.

"What's to stop someone from planting another bomb next week and asking for more money?" Bradley said, not really expecting Sistrunk to answer. "I mean, where does it end? I need some guarantees."

"I understand," Sistrunk said. "We hired Bello to find out ... "

"Well Mr. Bello may be a good investigator, but he may not be up to what it is I need done. That's the reason for this meeting. It's strictly business. You do what you have to do."

Now, on the deck of the Regal II, Bradley was reminding Scarpino of the deal they had struck six months earlier and of Scarpino's promise that the Renaissance would not have any problems from the underworld.

"Under the terms of our original agreement, you promised me this sort of thing would not happen. You also said if it did, you would take care of it."

"And I will," Scarpino said. "If it's coming from my world. But if this is some kind of payback for you and your company kissing up to the CIA and the Shah, then I have no obligation to do anything. Whadda I know or care about freakin' Muslims?"

Even Scarpino, whose lips moved when he read, had heard about the Renaissance giving shelter to the Shah after he was chased out of Iran.

"How do I know you guys ain't some front for the CIA?" Scarpino said, trying to take the offensive in the conversation. "Time Magazine said … "

"Mr. Scarpino, don't make me laugh. You know and I know that you don't read Time Magazine. Maybe you had someone read it to you, but let's not have a conversation here about geopolitics. It serves no purpose. Besides, we don't think the bomb threat came from any terrorist group or Islamic fundamentalist organization. Our friends in Washington assure us that the situation over there is so volatile no one would make a move like this."

"So where's that leave us?" Scarpino asked.

"We have someone coming into the casino tomorrow night. I may have some work for your people then. I assume you are capable of making someone talk when they'd prefer not to?"

"That won't be a problem."

Sistrunk was amazed at his boss. He didn't know Bradley had the guts to get in Scarpino's face the way he was. But then this had been a day of surprises.

On the ride out, Bradley had told him that he had been doing business with Scarpino for more than six months, that they had met like this once before to set up a real estate deal, a deal that Vinny Barbano had nixed, but that Scarpino had grabbed with both fists.

Scarpino set up a front company in the real estate business. Bradley was supplying the money. The company was buying up land all over the city, tying up development parcels left and right. The idea was to amass as much land as possible for future development while at the same time blocking other casinos from putting together land parcels large enough on which they could build.

It was a way for the Renaissance to limit its competition and control the overall, long-term development of the city.

The one glitch in the early planning stages of the deal was how they would get the money out of the casino to finance the land purchases. Then, by chance, Nicky Botts came to Scarpino with the hot dog scam and it all fell into place.

Botts thought he'd grab a quick 100 grand and fold the scam. Within a week he figured the two girls in the cashier's cage who were funneling the cash out to him would be found out and he'd have to run for cover. But Scarpino, after laying out the flimflam for Bradley, told Botts the deal was golden.

"We got somebody on the inside who will play with the books," Scarpino explained. "The missing money won't show up in the weekly accounting."

Botts was impressed.

So was Sistrunk, who was beginning to realize that corporate organized crime was where the real action was.

"We're the ones who took all the risk," Bradley had explained to Sistrunk. "We were the ones who worked

with the politicians and the unions, paid off the church-
es and the do-gooders to get the casino gambling referendum passed. We did all the work. We're the reason
casino gambling was legalized. And now these interlop-
ers, Resorts, Bally's, Caesars, these companies that
were afraid to take a chance, are gonna come in and
reap the benefits? I don't think so."

The deal was simple. Bradley supplied a tax map
with outlines around all the properties the Renaissance
Casinos Inc. wanted. He was looking for control of most
of the Boardwalk frontage zoned for casino gambling,
but he also wanted pieces in most of the adjacent blocks.

"If you can't build, at least you can block others from
assembling enough land to compete," he had said.

It was Monopoly played not on a game board, but on
the streets of Atlantic City. Bradley wanted to make sure
that Renaissance Casinos Inc. passed "Go" more often
than any of its competitors.

Fortune Realty was one of Scarpino's companies.
The deal he had struck with Bradley was good in both
the short and long term. Bradley set a price the compa-
ny was willing to pay for the properties it wanted. If
Scarpino could get them for less, he kept the difference.
That was the short-term benefit.

Scarpino's people had a way of persuading reluctant
property owners to sell, making them realize it was in
their best interest to get out.

Those who balked ended up with all kinds of
headaches. Health inspectors from the city, who were

on Scarpino's pad, would show up at restaurants and bars and cite them for code violations. Building inspectors would turn up at apartment houses and conduct random inspections, invariably finding problems with the electricity or the plumbing.

More than one property was firebombed. Residents would find their cars vandalized, the windows in their homes broken. It was slash and burn. After a few weeks of that, a salesman from Fortune would call back.

"We were just in the neighborhood," he would say, "and we were wondering if you've thought any more about our offer."

Long-term, the deal was even better. Scarpino was promised three points — a hidden 3 percent share — in any other casino Renaissance built in the city, as well as a guarantee that his companies, or companies he recommended, would get the service contracts. Linens, food and beverage, garbage collection. It meant millions.

Scarpino was sitting pretty. Everything was going according to plan.

Then somebody plants a bomb in the casino and on the same day Vinny Barbano gets popped.

"None of this is good for business," Scarpino said.

"I wholeheartedly agree," said G. Malcolm Bradley.

══════

"I'm telling ya, Scarpino had nothing to do with the Barbano hit," Nicky Botts said. "I'm sure of it."

Botts had been going on for nearly an hour. He was

sitting on a stool in the storage room of the discount store in black tuxedo pants and a white T-shirt that was soaked in sweat. His peanut shell body lay on the floor beside him.

Bello asked a few questions, but knew from past encounters that it was best to just let Botts tell the story his way.

After he blew the 39 grand, Botts said he had planned to throw himself at Scarpino's feet and ask for a second chance, promising to work the money off in other ways. That Monday night, before anyone even knew he had screwed up, he had gone to the Fairmount Tavern, where he knew Paulie Jr. hung out. He figured he'd work Scarpino's son first.

"You know how he is," Botts said. "Thinks he's a wiseguy. But if his father wasn't who he is, he'd be pushing a broom at Holy Spirit High School."

Paulie Jr. was drinking. And when he drank he talked more than he should. Botts used what he had left of the cash to buy round after round for the entire bar. By the end of the night, he had gotten the whole story out of young Paulie, who knew enough about the real estate deal his father had with the Renaissance to burst Botts' balloon.

"I think we got this scam and it turns out Scarpino's got it wired from the inside," Botts said, clearly upset at the propriety of it all. "We're getting all this money, but it ain't our money. He's using it to buy land for this Malcolm guy.

"Scarpino kept telling me my end was coming when we finished the scam. That I'd have a big payday. Payday my ass. My end was a .22. So now I know I can't go plead for mercy. I blew 39 large belonging to Paul Scarpino in four hours at the casino. He ain't gonna accept no explanations. I'm a dead man. So I left Paulie Jr. at the bar and went underground. But I can't live like this. That's why I called ya. Ya gotta get me in to see somebody. I wanna deal.

"I can give up all I know about the Scarpino organization. The scam with the casino, the real estate stuff. But I'm telling ya, Paulie Jr. said his father was a nervous wreck over the Barbano hit. Had no idea where it came from. Was worried he might be next. Swear to God, on my mother."

Bello told Botts he'd make a few calls, see what he could do.

"Let me check with Mike Quincy. He might like to hear what you have to say. And I know some people with the State Police who'd be very interested."

"Whatever you could do, Frankie, I appreciate."

Bello wasn't listening. His thoughts were going in another direction. If Scarpino wasn't behind the hit, who took out Vinny Barbano?

And who was behind the bomb threat and shake down of the Renaissance?

━━━

Bello stopped in the beauty parlor Saturday morning. He wanted to see Rita Manoff, wanted to ask her about some of the things Vinny Barbano had mentioned. See if he had ever spoken to her about them.

But when he got to the Casa di Coiffure, only Julia was working. She was cutting a customer's hair. Two others, a young man and an older woman, were reading magazines and waiting.

"Bello, how ya doin'?" Julia said with a smile. "Rita was looking for ya yesterday. You had an appointment, remember?"

Bello had forgotten.

"Christ, tell her I'm sorry. I got tied up. She gonna be around today?"

Julia put down her scissors and walked over to the appointments desk in the front of the shop. God, Bello thought, she was beautiful.

But there was something different about her today.

She caught him staring and smiled.

"Bello? What is it?"

He liked the way she called him 'Bello.' It was familiar, like she had been doing it for years, like they were comfortable with each other.

"I don't know," he said. "I'm trying to figure that out."

"It's my hair," she said. "Jesus, for somebody who gets paid to investigate and observe, you ain't much, are you? Rita cut it yesterday. Too short?"

Her hair, which had flowed down to the middle of her back, was now cropped at her neckline. It was still thick and dark but considerably shorter than it had been. He liked it. It made her other features more pronounced, brought out the high cheekbones, the wide mouth, the full lips. Bello stopped short again.

"What's with you today, Bello?" Julia said.

"Sorry, I got a lot on my mind. So, is Rita coming back today?"

"No, she said she was making some travel plans. I think she's gonna take a trip. What with Vinny and now she's sold her house, I think she's tired"

"Sold the house?"

"You didn't know? She's had it on the market for months. She'll probably move upstairs. One thing's for sure, she ain't selling this joint. Had another big blowout on the phone yesterday with that real estate guy from Fortune Realty."

Julia turned the pages in the appointment book.

"Look, I can pencil you in for Monday morning, 10 a.m. How's that?"

"Great," Bello said. "I didn't know you cut hair, too."

"Bello, there's a lot you don't know about me," she said with an easy smile.

He turned toward the door, then paused and turned back.

"Listen," he said. "Would you like to have dinner sometime?"

"Yeah, Bello, I would."

"Good. Tonight's out cause I gotta be somewhere, but maybe one night next week?"

"Tonight's not good for me either. I'm going to visit my mother in Philly. But yeah, call me next week ... or let me know when you come in Monday. All right? Don't forget, Bello. I'll tell Rita you were here."

═════

They were all sitting in the 12th floor office when the gambler showed up at the baccarat table. There was a bank of television screens in Bradley's office linked to the security system. Eye-in-the-sky cameras mounted in the ceiling of the casino could home in on any location on the casino floor and transmit the pictures back to the televisions in the executive suite. The technology was so good you could zero in on a dealer's fingers. Practically take his prints.

Sistrunk, Bradley and Bello had been watching and waiting for 20 minutes. Bradley had told Sistrunk he wanted Bello there.

"I strikes me that Mr. Bello has too much of a conscience," Bradley said to Sistrunk.

"You got that right," Sistrunk said.

"Exactly. So I want to know where he is when we do what we have to do. Make sure he's here with us. I don't want him out on the casino floor getting in the way."

"I'll see to it."

Bello was surprised by the invitation to the executive suite. He had planned to watch the action from the bar just off the baccarat pit and then follow the gambler. Now he'd have an even better view. He figured he could get down to the casino floor before the night was over and pick up the tail before his target headed out.

In the one phone call, the extortionist had said that

his "representative" would arrive around 8 p.m. and would be wearing a black suit over a dark turtle-neck shirt.

No one figured it would be a woman.

"Damn," Bello said. "They keep surprising us."

She had long blonde hair and wore sunglasses that covered the top half of her face. She was heavily made up with rouge and dark lipstick.

And she was cool as ice.

She lit a cigarette, slid $5,000 onto the table for chips and started playing. The security camera zeroed in on her hands from time and time. Bello thought there was something familiar in the way they moved.

There was a confidence in her manner. Her actions were almost second nature.

Bradley and Sistrunk had arranged for three dealers to work the table that night. They would rotate 30-minute shifts. The dealers were told to manipulate the deck, which any good dealer could do. However the gambler bet, that's the way the cards would spin out.

She started out betting with $500 chips. By the time the third dealer started his first rotation, she was laying $10,000 on each hand. Within four hours, she had won $4 million. She never stopped for a drink. Never asked for a bathroom break.

It was an incredible display of stamina.

Bello was impressed.

The casino was jammed. Wall to wall people. Hardly anyone noticed. At midnight when the woman stood up and signaled that she was ready to cash out, G. Malcolm Bradley reached for the phone.

He quickly punched four digits. He was calling someone in the hotel.

"She's heading out. Remember. First you get the information, then you do whatever you want."

Bello looked at Sistrunk.

"What's that about?" he said, his voice rising.

G. Malcolm Bradley interrupted.

"Mr. Bello, your services are no longer required."

As he said this, Bradley was writing out a check.

"Six days, $2,400," he said. "I've added an extra $600 to make it an even three grand. I hope that's satisfactory?"

Bello looked at Sistrunk, then at Bradley.

"Who'd you just call?"

"Let it go, Bello," Sistrunk said. "You gotta stop being a fuckin' Boy Scout. This doesn't concern you. Take the money and go. You do the right thing here, there'll be more work for you in the future."

Bello left the check and headed for the door. He took the elevator down to the lobby and headed for the cashier's cage. It had taken a mere five minutes for the woman to sign the necessary papers for the wire transfer. Once the confirmation came back that the money had been received by the Swiss bank, she was on her way. Cool as ever, the woman was already walking toward the exit doors that opened onto Pennsylvania Avenue when Bello spotted her.

Then he saw them, falling in line behind her. The Prato brothers, Matty and Marc. Scarpino's goons.

Bello broke into a trot. When he reached the exit door he saw the woman getting into a taxi. A dark Lincoln pulled out of the shadows and the two mobsters jumped in. The Lincoln headed out after the cab.

Bello brushed past a couple who reeked of smoke and booze and jumped into the taxi they had hailed.

"I wanna go where that Lincoln's going," he said.

Chapter 7

T he taxi with the blonde headed down Pennsylvania Avenue and made a left onto Atlantic. The Lincoln with the Prato brothers screeched through a yellow warning light. Frank Bello's taxi ran the red.

The three vehicles continued south on Atlantic Avenue, joining the flow of cars, taxis, limos and buses that continued to shuttle people to and from the only casino in town.

The Renaissance Casino Hotel was a beacon of light and activity in an Atlantic City that was still in the very early stages of the "unique form of urban renewal" that the casino gambling advocates had promised.

In fact, the early stages looked a lot like any one of New Jersey's many troubled cities. Take away the Renaissance Casino and Atlantic City circa 1979 was a mirror image of Newark or Paterson or Jersey City or Camden.

As they headed past New York Avenue, Bello saw two hookers fighting with what looked like their pimp outside the "All-Night All Nude" go-go lounge. The lounge, which had been open two months, was one of the city's newest businesses. A grand opening sign — "two drinks for the price of one" — was still mounted over the flashing neon sign that blinked "all nude, all nice." It was not exactly the kind of trickle-down economic development that casino proponents had been promising. But it certainly was another example of the big hustle the city had become.

Everybody was grabbing for a piece of the action. The blonde and her extortion partners had just scored $4 million from the Renaissance Casino Hotel. Matty and Marc Prato, Scarpino's goons, were now looking to get the money back and find out who was behind the shakedown.

And Frankie Bello?

Bello wasn't sure why, but he knew he had to finish what he had started. That's what had made him a good cop and a good private investigator. It's also what had forced him to quit the department and what kept him scrounging for paydays in the private sector.

"You have to go along to get along," Sistrunk had preached when they were both working for the detective squad. "When are you going to learn? When are you going to stop being a Boy Scout?"

Sistrunk had cashed in. Bello was sure Sistrunk was in the middle of all that was playing out right now.

He was also certain that Scarpino had some kind of relationship with Bradley. Why else would Scarpino's muscle be after the people who scammed Bradley's casino? With Vinny Barbano out of the picture, Scarpino was positioned to take over the city. A secret working relationship with the top casino executive on the Boardwalk would only enhance his position.

So was the Barbano hit tied to the casino scam? Bello knew it had to be. He was also sure that the blonde in the taxi that was now pulling into the Atlantic City train terminal could tell him how and why.

He just had to get to her first.

And that would require getting past Matty and Marc.

———

There was a time when Frankie Bello went up against the Prato brothers every day. This was back when they were in high school. Bello usually ended up eating dirt.

The Pratos were seniors when he was a sophomore at Holy Spirit. Matty Prato was a defensive end on the football team. Made All-South Jersey and All-Catholic his senior year. Marc Prato was a middle linebacker. He was All-Catholic and third team All-South Jersey.

They were both tenacious. Played with what the coach liked to call "reckless abandon." This meant that they were both a little bit nuts.

The Pratos were 16 months apart in age, but their mother had held Matty out of school one year so the boys would be in the same grade.

Each was 6-foot-3 and, during their playing days,

weighed in at around 220. Bello figured they were up around 250 or 260 now.

Their mother named them after the saints who wrote the gospels. Both had the same middle name, Alphonse. This came from their father. He wanted to honor his hero. Al Capone.

The Pratos won scholarships to Villanova. But within a year they were both back home. Each blew out a different knee. That ended their football careers and without football, they saw no need for academia.

When they came back to Atlantic City they went to work for Scarpino's construction company. Little Paulie was a friend of their old man's. They worked for the cement company, laying rebar. It only made them tougher. They were like rocks. Eventually, Scarpino found a more suitable line of work for the Pratos.

They became headbusters, enforcers. Whenever Scarpino had some dirty work, he would send Matty and Marc. Usually, they got the job done.

Bello cringed at the thought of going up against them. He remembered how they would pound him into the ground every day after school during football practice. Then they would help him up and smile.

By the end of the year, he was bruised and bloody, but had earned their respect.

"You ain't a bad guy, Bello," they said. "You take a beatin' and you don't complain. You got heart."

That might not be enough this time.

Bello, from the back seat of the cab, saw the blonde

get out of her taxi in front of the train station. Trains ran to Philadelphia and New York every hour. It was a quarter to one in the morning. The Lincoln pulled up almost immediately after the blonde had disappeared through the train station doors. The Pratos sprung out of the back seat. Bello, jumping from his taxi before it had even stopped, was right on them.

"Yo, Matty," he said.

Both brothers turned around.

"Go, go," Matty said to Marc. "I'll take care of this."

Marc headed into the terminal. Matty blocked Bello, who tried to follow.

"Frankie, this is got nuthin' to do wit you," Matty said as he placed a huge arm around Bello's shoulders and guided him into an alley.

Midway up the alley and far enough from the street that no one could see or hear what was going on, Matty stopped.

"We were told to look out for ya," he said. "How do you wanna do this?"

"Matty, do you know what you're doing?"

"I'm doin' what I'm told," he said. "I'm doin' what I'm paid to do."

Bello tried to fake right and slip by Matty on the left. But the move, which seldom worked on the football field, was futile in the alley. Matty stuck out an arm and clothes-lined Bello, cracking him in the Adam's apple. Bello gagged and fell. Matty picked him up and delivered a right to the stomach. Then two more stunning shots to his rib cage. Bello felt the air rush out of his body. He couldn't breathe. Matty came with another right, this one alongside Bello's cheek. He felt his eye socket explode. He saw stars as his body slammed up against a brick wall, then slowly slid down in a heap. As he looked up, he saw Matty Prato breaking into a trot and heading back toward the terminal.

Bello struggled to pull himself up. He fell down twice before making it to an erect position. His face was throbbing. His throat was raw. His ribs were killing him. Every breath sent a shooting pain up his left side.

He staggered out of the alley and fell into Mike Quincy who was getting out of a squad car. Six other uniformed officers were piling out of a police van that pulled up behind him.

"Jesus, Bello, what happened to you?" Quincy said.

"Inside, Quince, the Prato brothers."

Quincy signaled to a sergeant who was heading the squad of uniforms.

"I got this frantic call from a cab driver. Said you tipped him fifty bucks and told him to call me direct. Since he had my home number, I knew he had to be for real. What's going on?"

"Quince, not now. Lemme sort this out. Just get the Pratos outta here. When I know more, you'll know more."

"Look, Bello, I owe ya. Nicky Botts has been singing for two days now. So I'll give ya this. But I want your word that I'm gonna hear from ya."

"You got it," Bello said.

Bello and Quincy walked through the train station doors and onto the floor of the terminal just as the uniforms were putting cuffs on the Pratos. The sergeant hustled over to Quincy.

"Whadda we got?" Quincy said.

"Not much," said the sergeant. "Marc was telling big Matty here that some woman was in the bathroom. Then when he saw us, he clammed up. Now all they're saying is they wanna speak to their lawyers."

Quincy turned toward Bello.

"Frankie?"

"Let it go for now, Mike. I'll fill ya in later."

The Pratos glared at Bello as they were led past him in handcuffs.

Even though his head was throbbing and his ribs felt like they had caved in, Bello forced a smile.

"You probably ought to get to the emergency room," Quincy said. "Want us to give you a lift?"

"Nah," said Bello. "I gotta take care of something here first."

Bello looked toward the women's restroom.

"I'll get back to ya. My word. On my mother."

Quincy headed out the door.

Bello walked slowly toward the horseshoe-shaped bar in the corner of the terminal. He took a stool with a clear view of the door leading to the women's restroom. Then he ordered a beer.

He figured he blacked out. Didn't know how long, but could tell he had lost consciousness. His head was resting in his arms on the bar.

And Julia was standing beside him.

"Bello, are you OK?"

"What?"

"Are you okay? What happened to you?

She reached up and touched his eye. It was black and blue and swollen shut.

"It's nothing," he said. "Ran into a door. What are you doing here?"

"I just got back from Philly," she said. "I was at my mom's for dinner. She had half the family there. I thought I was never gonna get back."

She was wearing jeans, sneakers and a Rutgers College sweatshirt. She had a small leather carry-all bag over her shoulder. Her hair looked as if it had just been blown dry. It was all fluffy and a little wild. Her face was scrubbed clean, hardly any make-up. Just a hint of lipstick.

"I just came out of the ladies room," she said. "If I hadn't stopped there, I probably would have walked right past you. Are you sure you're OK?"

Mention of the ladies' room cleared his head.

"Did you see anybody in there, a blonde with long hair and sunglasses?"

Julia feigned anger.

"Bello I'm away for three hours and you're trolling

the train station for blondes?"

He tried to smile but his face hurt too much. Then he tried to stand up, but sunk quickly back onto the stool, his head spinning.

Julia stood up, put his arm over her shoulder and helped him up.

"Come on. I'm taking you home."

———

Nicky Botts was working on his second piece of pizza smothered in anchovies.

"How can you eat that stuff?" the state police detective asked. "I'm gagging over here just looking at it."

"You don't know what good is," Botts said. "I never met a cop yet who knew how to eat. You guys think meatloaf and mashed potatoes is cuisine. Fuckin' 'medigans. We got any more beer?"

"Easy on the beer," Quincy said. "We wanna get two more hours out of you today. You could have all you want at dinner tonight."

It was Sunday afternoon. Quincy had been up all night processing the Prato arrests, but he wasn't tired. IIe was going on pure adrenaline, which had kicked in during the excitement at the train station and was now in overdrive as he heard more and more from Botts.

Botts had met with Quincy Friday afternoon. Bello set it up. Quincy brought the State Police and attorney general's office into it once he heard what Botts had to say. The state had more resources and knew the drill when it came to protecting witnesses.

Two State Police detectives and a deputy attorney general had been camping out with Botts since Friday night in a condominium in Cape May. It was the off-season so they had the town to themselves. Quincy drove down each day to see how things were going.

"I wanna go back to the restaurant where we ate last night," Botts said.

They had eaten at Spiaggia, a fancy joint right on the ocean. During the summer season you had to wait an hour or more for a table. During the off-season, it was open on weekends and much easier to get a seat. Any time of the year, the food was great.

"Whatever you want, Nick," Quincy said. "The state's picking up the tab. Just stay focused for now. We need a little more information."

There was a tape recorder on the table in front of Botts. A pile of tapes already labeled and cross-referenced were stacked next to the recorder. Botts had talked for 12 hours over two days and still wasn't finished.

The deputy attorney general, a guy named Paul Jordan, was already drawing up arrest warrants for Scarpino, the Prato brothers, Paulie Scarpino Jr., Sistrunk and G. Malcolm Bradley. Jordan had had to clear the last two with the attorney general who, in turn, had had to call the governor. Surprisingly, the word came back that it was all a go.

"Bradley's pissed a lot of people off with his arrogance," Jordan explained to Quincy. "Now with Resorts about to open and Bally's and Caesars World in the wings, I think the governor wants to send a little message to the Renaissance people."

"Fuckin' politics," Botts said, as he reached for a third slice. "How about a Coke, at least?"

"Sure," Quincy said. "But let's go over the scam one more time."

Botts, who loved talking about himself, jumped at the chance to tell the story again.

"There was these two broads I was partying with," he said. "Young girls, but sophisticated, ya know?"

Quincy rolled his eyes and looked at Jordan who was trying not to laugh.

"I hear ya," Quincy said.

"So we're talking, this and that, and I find out they both work for the casino, in the cashier's cage at the Renaissance."

From there Botts explained how he arranged to show up twice each day with a wad of cash from his hot dog stand and how he would ask for 200 $1 bills.

"See, the broads had rigged a couple of piles of $100 bills," he said to Jordan, realizing Quincy already knew the details. "They'd slide those stacks out. They had slipped dollar bill wrappers around 100 dollar bill stacks. They put a $1 bill on the top and bottom of each stack. It was beautiful. Twice a day I'm taking twenty grand out of the casino."

Then Botts' face turned angry and he began to talk

even faster than he normally did. Looking directly at Jordan he explained how he had blown the thirty-nine grand gambling at the casino; how he found out that Scarpino had the deal wired from inside; how Scarpino and Bradley were working their own scam on him.

"I'm thinking we're stockpiling this money and this motherfucker Scarpino is using it to buy property for this other motherfucker Bradley," Botts said. "Can you fuckin' believe it? They're trying to buy the whole city. With *my* money. And I ain't gettin' a piece of this action."

With that, Botts picked up another slice of pizza, then slammed it back onto the table.

"Not a fuckin' piece."

Jordan was scribbling furiously on a yellow legal pad as the tape recorder continued to roll.

"Racketeering, conspiracy, real estate fraud, unlawful conveyance, embezzlement. It just keeps getting better and better," the state prosecutor said.

"Now can we go eat?" asked Nicky Botts.

Chapter 8

Frankie Bello woke up in his own bed with the smell of coffee coming out of the kitchen. His clothes from the night before were neatly folded over a chair. His wallet, keys and a wad of cash were on the nightstand.

He looked around the room, trying to remember what had happened. His ribs still ached, but not as bad as before. His left eye was still swollen shut.

He heard the shower running in the bathroom. Then it stopped. Julia came out wearing his terry cloth robe, towel-drying her hair.

"Bello," she said with a smile that gave him butterflies. "I thought you were gonna sleep all morning. I got coffee on in the kitchen. I also made you a pot of chicken soup. Gotta tell ya, Bello, you ain't much for provisions. I hadda run to the deli next door."

"What happened?" Bello said. "How did I get here?"

"I can't talk now, Bello. I'm late. I gotta open the shop. Rita's still not back. The soup is in a pot on the stove. Just heat it up when you're ready. Eat a big bowl;

it'll make you feel better. It's got escarole in it, but I did-n't have time to make the little meatballs."

"Did you spend the night?"

"No, I came over this morning for a shower," she said sarcastically. "Of course I spent the night. You got a problem with that?"

Bello laughed. God she was beautiful.

"How was it?" he said.

"There's a lot we gotta work on, Bello. So far we just got the sleeping part down."

With that she threw the towel at him, slipped out of the robe and pulled on the jeans and sweatshirt that he now remembered she had been wearing the night before — actually earlier that morning — in the train station.

"Tomorrow morning, Bello. Ten o'clock. You got an appointment with me. Don't forget."

Then she was gone.

Bello got up, had a cup of coffee and quickly went back to bed. He awoke around three. Heated the soup, which smelled delicious, and ate a huge bowl with a half of a loaf of day-old Italian bread. Then he showered, dressed and walked outside to sit in the sun for a few hours. He was tired and confused.

He got a call around 7 p.m. He hoped it was Julia, but it was Quincy.

"Watch the news tomorrow morning," was all Quincy said before hanging up the phone.

The next morning Bello felt surprisingly better. His

ribs still ached, but he could breathe without the shooting pain. His cheek was black and blue, but the swelling
around his eye had gone down quite a bit. As he was
shaving, he turned on the radio, switching to the all-
news station.

He caught the tail-end of the report about the
arrests of "mob kingpin Paul 'Little Paulie' Scarpino,
casino mogul G. Malcolm Bradley, and several of their
top associates, including former Atlantic City Police
Captain Thomas Sistrunk." They were charged with
scamming hundreds of thousands of dollars out of the
casino to finance a real estate speculation scheme that
included extortion and arson for hire.

Bello was impressed. Quincy and the State Police
had done a lot in 48 hours. Both he and Quincy agreed
that Sistrunk would roll once he spent a night behind
bars. His testimony, if he agreed to cooperate, would
make the case even stronger.

The news report ended with speculation that
Scarpino was also suspected in the "gangland slaying of
reputed mob boss Vinny Barbano." It was the only part
of the story that Bello wasn't sure about. But he intended to find out.

———

Frankie Bello walked the Boards to New York
Avenue, about two miles. The salt air and the sun
revived him. All the while he kept going over his last
conversation with Vinny Barbano. It was hard to believe
it had been only a week. Last Monday he met with

Barbano in the beauty salon. Now he was heading back there to find out who had killed the mob boss.

"Scarpino is a stupid, greedy man," Barbano had said. "He knows nothing about This Thing of Ours. You may not agree, but this is a thing of honor. There was a time when that meant something. Today, I'm not so sure."

"What does Scarpino have to do with any of this?" said Bello who had told Barbano about the bomb threat and the extortion note at the casino.

But Barbano ignored the question.

"The man who hired you, Bradley? He's got no integrity. We're the gangsters? He's organized crime. He and his kind bring a cancer to the city. And the state, the governor, the legislators, the attorney general, they all open their arms and say welcome. Come right in. How can we help you?"

Bello was confused.

"I don't follow," he said.

"Several months ago," Barbano said. "I had a call from Mr. Bradley. We met over dinner in Spring Lake, out of the way. He came with a proposition, which I rejected. He wants to own the city, control all the development. Later, I found out he brought the same proposal to Scarpino. Needless to say, Scarpino could not turn it down. He was blinded by the money."

Vinny Barbano had sighed like a man who was both tired and disappointed.

"Twenty years ago there would have been a way to

deal with Scarpino and Bradley," he said. "They would have been squashed like bugs. But that's not the way things are done now. So you look for other ways to deal with the problem. There are things, at this point, you're better off not knowing. Believe me. When the time is right, come back and see me again. If I can fill in the blanks, I'll be happy to do so."

Two hours later, Barbano's Lincoln went up in flames and so did any chance Bello had of asking the old mob boss any more questions.

———

Julia came up and kissed Bello on the cheek when he walked into the beauty parlor.

"I got a chair ready for ya," she said. "You look good, hell of a lot better than yesterday. How'd ya sleep? Didja eat the soup?"

Bello grabbed Julia by both hands.

"It's good to see you, too," he said. "But I'm the one who's going to be asking the questions this morning."

"Is that so?" she said.

"It is," he said.

Bello walked over to the chair and sat down. Julia wrapped a plastic cover around his chest and shoulders and then tilted the chair back so that his head was over the sink. She turned on the water, got the temperature right and began to shampoo.

It felt great. As she massaged, Bello closed his eyes. He could get used to this.

"What is it that you want to know, Bello?" she said

softly.

"Everything," he replied.

Julia rinsed his hair, then brought the chair back into an upright position. She took out her clippers and began to comb and snip.

"That's a tall order," she said.

"I got lots of time and nowhere to go," Bello replied.

"Tell ya what, Bello. Rita left you a letter. It's over there by the counter. I'll finish cutting your hair. You take the letter. Read it. Then come back tonight and I'll answer all your questions.

"We'll have dinner upstairs. I'll make us two nice steaks with portabella mushrooms and a little *cima di rabe* on the side. You bring some bread and a bottle of wine."

Bello started to protest, but Julia put her hand softly on his lips. Then she leaned in close.

"Are you a good listener Bello?" she said, her lips now brushing against his ear. "Because if you are, we'll still be talking about it over breakfast in the morning."

━━━

Bello sat on a bench in the sun on the Boardwalk reading and re-reading the letter Rita Manoff had left for him.

"The city's not the same without Vinny. I know you understand. There are certain people who, from the very moment you meet, become a part of you. That's the way it was for Vinny and me. Frankie, I've seen the way you look at Julia and the way she looks at you. You could have a good thing if you just let it happen.

"I'm going to do some traveling. I hope to visit Italy. Vinny always talked about the town where his parents were born and so I think I will spend some time there.

"If you need to reach me, I will be at this address.

"Love, Rita"

She then wrote the street name and number for a condominium apartment in Lecce, in the province of Puglia in southern Italy.

Bello knew nothing about the city or the province. But the street address jumped off the page. It was Seventeen Via Duca D'Osta. The address was neatly hand printed. There was a little curly line through the middle of the seven. Bello had seen the printing and the number once before, a week earlier as he sat in G. Malcom Bradley's office on the 12th floor of the Renaissance Casino Hotel reading the extortion note.

———

Bello woke up Tuesday morning with Julia lying naked in bed next to him. He had to meet with Quincy at the police administration building at noon. He had promised to tell him all he knew about the mysterious blonde and the $4 million ripoff at the baccarat table. Bello decided he would give up what he could. The blonde, he would say, had disappeared that night, which she had. And, at the time, he had no idea who she was.

Now he knew she was lying in bed next to him, but it was not something he planned to share with Quincy.

Over dinner the night before, Julia had laid it all out

for him.

"Vinny wanted out and this was his way of doing it," she said. "He knew Scarpino was in business with Bradley and figured it was only a matter of time before one of the New York families backed Scarpino."

Bello remembered his last conversation with Barbano and how the mob boss had said the same thing, although not in so many words.

"He didn't want to go to war," she said. "He said it wasn't worth it. And he knew if he stayed, either he'd have to kill Scarpino or Scarpino would have to kill him. So he figured he'd make one big score, tweak Bradley and Scarpino in the process, and then get out. He never figured it would end with them getting arrested, but I doubt he would be upset about it.

"You were a bonus," Julia added.

"Oh?" Bello said.

"Absolutely. In fact, when you came to see him that morning at the beauty parlor he was beside himself. After you left, he was smiling from ear to ear. He told Rita and me that you would be the perfect foil for Bradley. He said he knew Bradley would try to play you, but that you'd see through it.

"He said you were a brickheaded Calabrese who never let anyone tell you what to do or how to think. He also said you were someone who knew what was right and what was wrong. He said you had heart. Is that so, Bello?"

Bello took a sip of the wine.

"I'm only half Calabrese, on my father's side," he said finally. "My mother was Sicilian."

"That's not what I meant."

They were quiet for a while. Bello complimented her on the steak and mushrooms. He poured some more wine.

She seemed to be comfortable just sitting at the table with him.

"Turns out he was right," Julia said. "You were gonna save me that night ... . And you didn't even know it was me."

Bello took another sip of the wine, then stared at the young woman sitting at the table across from him. God, she was beautiful, he thought.

They made love right after dessert and again before climbing into bed to sleep.

Now, as he sat next to her, he wondered what he would tell Mike Quincy. Certainly not what he had learned; the scam at the casino was Vinny Barbano's big hustle and he had left the city a better place for it.

Scarpino and Bradley were off the streets and out of business. The casino regulators had shown some muscle. And the anti-casino advocates had a little more clout. Not that they would be able to change anything, but at least when they complained, the powers that be might be more inclined to listen.

Maybe this unique form of urban renewal had a shot after all.

As Bello sat in Julia's bed, he was looking directly at

the blonde wig and the sunglasses. That was another part of the story Quincy would not be hearing. He also figured he'd leave out the fact that Julia's second cousin worked the night shift at the city morgue and that he was the guy, the *chiadrule*, who called in about the missing body after Barbano was killed. Some things were better left unsaid.

"He was a John Doe," Julia explained. "We had to wait until someone like that turned up. He was about Vinny's age and size. They found him dead under the Boardwalk. No one claimed the body."

"What happens now?" Bello had asked.

"That depends on you," Julia said. "Rita's left me the business and the apartment. She's supposed to send a check each month, my end of the take.

"She also said I get to keep you."

"She did," Bello said, starting to smile. "And what have I got to say about that?"

"Bello, you got nothing to say in the matter. You were done that first day, when I caught you staring at me in the mirror."

"You really are beautiful," Bello said.

Julia just smiled.

━━━━

Bello spent about an hour meeting with Quincy the afternoon. He told him all the details about the casino extortion; the bomb left under the baccarat table, the note, the phone call and the rigged baccarat game that was used to make the payoff.

"The blonde was the woman the Pratos were chasing that night at the train station," Bello said. "I figure she was catching a train to Philadelphia or New York. God knows where she is now."

"You think it's connected with the Barbano hit?" Quincy asked.

"Seems probable," Bello said, "but I got a feeling this is one of those gangland killings that never gets solved."

"You sure there's not more you wanna tell me?" said Quincy.

"On my mother," Bello said in complete honesty. "I have no idea who killed Vinny Barbano."

———

Rita Manoff had taken the Monday night Alitalia flight out of Newark International Airport. She arrived in Rome a little before 8 a.m. Tuesday morning. After passing through Customs, she caught another flight down to Brindisi and then, as she had been told, took the bus from the airport to Lecce, a 50-minute ride through the sun-dappled olive groves and flat farmland of southern Italy.

The bus pulled onto the Viale Garibaldi and rumbled to a stop in front the sprawling, tree-lined Gardino Pubblico in the center of the city. It was a little after 1 p.m. Rita, tired but happy, was one of the last passengers to step off the bus. The first person she saw was Tony the Brute. He was standing in the shade, looking at the pictures in L'Espresso, the Italian news magazine. Sitting on a bench near the Brute was a well-dressed and neatly groomed man in his late 50s or early 60s. It was hard to tell. He was holding a bouquet of flowers and when he saw Rita, his deeply tanned face broke into a warm and radiant smile.

"*Cara mia*," he said as he stood to greet her. "Welcome to Lecce. The most beautiful city in all of Italy."

"Vinny," Rita said. "You look good for a dead man."

About the Author

Veteran Inquirer reporter George Anastasia started writing about the mob while working in the paper's Atlantic City bureau in 1976 — the year New Jersey voters approved legalized gambling.

Photo / CLIFF MAUTNER

He has also written for several national magazines and is the author of four books of non-fiction.

His last, *The Summer Wind,* was an account of the Thomas Capano-Anne Marie Fahey murder case, a story he covered in depth for The Inquirer. His other books, all dealing with the Philadelphia mob, are *The Goodfella Tapes, Mobfather* and *Blood and Honor,* which Jimmy Breslin called "the best gangster book ever written."

Born in South Philadelphia, Anastasia grew up in southern New Jersey. He is a graduate of Dartmouth College and has taught as an adjunct professor at Rowan University and Temple University. He joined The Inquirer in 1974.

He and his wife reside in Gloucester County.